A Whale of a Good Time

Poems and Paintings by Theresa LaBrecque

Published 2008 by Mermaid Publishing Grotto

Art © 2006 –2008 by Theresa LaBrecque

Poems © 2008 by Theresa LaBrecque

Edited by Colleen Perry

Printed in Hong Kong

Theresa LaBrecque: theresa@thecapecodmermaid.com

ISBN 978-0-9794820-1-4

A Whale of a Good Time

A Whale of a Garden

On this whale there grows a rose.
A rose, a rose,
Sweetness in every petal,
Fragrance for the nose.
And on this rose there grows a thorn.
A thorn, a thorn,
Protector of the rose.
And so my dear, it grows,
And grows
A sweet and tender rose.

3

4

Bewitched Whale

Should pity be extended?
A whale so offended?
A ride, a display of jack-o'-lanterns.
Their beauty from wick it burns
And offers a gilded retreat.
Rest for the poor witch's feet.
Rest after the long hallow's night,
For one who's job it is to fright
On this scary autumn night!

Cat Nap

My mother could sleep here.
She could sleep anywhere,
On waves gently rising
With cats, so surprising,
Gently rocked to sleep
On colored waves of the deep.

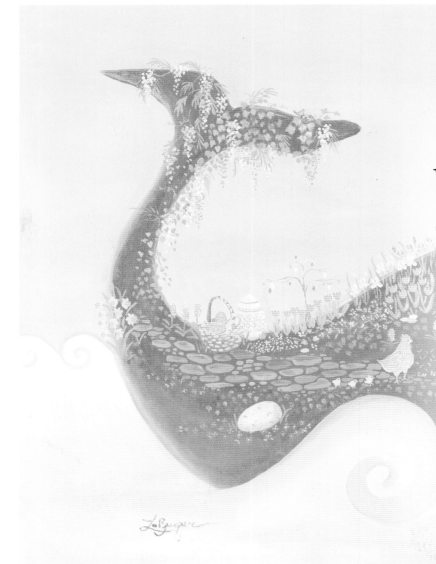

Easter Whale

Tulips, irises and daffodils—
Pink bunnies and all the frills.
Hidden eggs from youthful eyes.
Hippity – hoppity skies.
Pink, blue, sea-foam green,
Lavender and yellow seen.
Jellybeans hidden all over the place.
Warm loving smiles on grandmother's face.
Pretty Easter baskets filled with sweets
This spring day is a welcome treat!

Valentine

Whale you be mine?
Oh my dear valentine,
So grand is my love for you
It will take a whale or two.
Like an airplane banner.
I will tell you in this manner,
Of my love so true.
Written over the ocean blue
On a whale so obliging
To be covered in writing,
Love notes from me to you.

Nothing Like It

Wait! Wait! Before you go
For sun-bathing you must know!
I must tell you of the best—
A place so special to sun and rest.
It's true! It's true! I put it to the test.
For sure, it's the back of a great big whale!
I know, I know, but it's not a tale.
Nothing like it. Sunning is best on a whale!

Afternoon Tea

Yum! Afternoon tea for you and me,
Out here on waves of the sea.
Mermaid and whale, with much to say.
Will anyone join us today?
All are welcome to our tea.
Invitations were tossed into the sea,
Tucked in old bottles and set afloat.
Will our guests arrive on a boat?
Or will they catch a ride on a fin?
A fin of orca or dolphin?
Swim, fly or catch a ride!
Of this I must confide—
Tea on a whale with mermaid, too,
Will not soon be forgotten by me or you!

14

Wedding Bells Ring

Wedding bells ring
Ding-o-ling
In the middle of the big blue sea.
They ring, they ring for you and me!
They shout it out for all to hear.
Come! It's time to gather near.
Whales, dolphins, sea turtles too,
Come to witness this love so true.
Gifts bought for giving
Meet their needs for living.
What a privilege this ceremony
Mermaid and merman in holy matrimony.

17

18

Snowmen Afloat

Snowflakes dance down from the sky.
And listen, because I do not lie.
I saw this, bizarre but it's true,
I saw a mermaid on the ocean blue.
She sat on a whale, dressed in winter fur.
I know what I saw—it was not a bur.
She made snowmen and snowwomen too.
It was then I knew I had to tell you!
I saw that she blessed them and set them afloat.
I witnessed this scene—safe from my boat.

Seafairing Cowboy

Whoa-hoa-hoa
Whee-hee-hee
This wave riding whale
Definitely for me!
One minute the sky—
The next the sea!
Whoa-hoa-hoa
Whee-hee-hee
A wave riding cowboy—that's me!

21

Ghost Ship Whale

Sit right down and I'll tell you a tale.

A true and sad tale of a ghost ship whale.

You see, they went out to hunt her,

Those pirates of the land down under.

Many harpoons flew in the sky!

And one, poor thing, got her in the eye.

In a splash the battle was over

When she rose from the waves and took the ship over!

I heard she vowed never to set them free

They live there now doomed at sea.

24

Serenity Whale

Here on my whale with flowers, birds and bees
I have no concerns to worry me
I want to be here and meditate
Rest my soul and rejuvenate.
This gentle whale sings to me.
She scribes her songs into my memory.
Sweet gentleness and love abound.
Sunbeams, butterflies and beauty surround.
Here my mind settles in sweet serenity.
Please…embrace the whale and follow me.

Santa's Rest

If I were tired Santa in need of rest
I would have a few places I love best.
Like the back of a whale,
Making a pillow of his tail
I would catch a few z's
While we floated at sea.
The whale's song my lullaby—
This is something you should try.
Close your eyes and be with me.
Use your imagination and smell the sea.

28

Swing on Whaleback Hill

Just imagine, if you will,
A beautiful swing on Whaleback Hill.
Covered in ivy and rose,
Some sit on it and pose.
Not I. I choose to fly!
Up…up…up to the sky!
Then down…down…down to the sea!

To be Irish

Humble clovers worn with pride,
Shades of green have all been tried
To convey this love content.
To be Irish—a whimsical event!
Leprechauns, mermaids, and fairies too
Banshees with curses to frighten you.
In Irish waters whales have been seen.
Listen to this!... they wore shades of green!

Sailor's Delight

Red sunset at night,
Sailor's delight
Red sun in the morning,
Sailor takes warning.
Over the years this poem has been told
So you will take heed and grow old.

Library Whale

Book mobile of the sea,
Will you bring a book to me?
Can you find my neighborhood,
That I might borrow Robin Hood?

May I then read this treasure
On your back in sweet leisure?
Your back…it really is such fun
When reading here with everyone!

Walrus reading Alice's Wonderland.
Look! An octopus with book in hand!
Penguins…they are huddled here
'Midst maids with starfish in their hair.

Many books I must borrow.
Please come back for me tomorrow.

Fourth of July

In the deepest, blackest, night,
There rose from the whale, starry light.
Fireworks with magic untold!
Wow! What a wonder to behold!
Feelings of patriotism flew to my chest—
Red, white and blue, I know as best.
Love for my country filled me from head to toe.
Now the grand finale! It's time to go.

Circus Dogs

Circus dogs on a whale—
Who would believe such a tale?
Dogs ever so eager to please,
And one just to be silly and tease.
Daily acts entertain you.
Fun on a whale? Who knew?
Popcorn? Peanuts? Coke?
If you tell anyone they'll think it a joke.

Artist Me

Artist me, out here on the peaceful rolling sea,
I have asked some whales to come and pose for me.
Canvases and paint await a masterpiece to create.
Hoping, of course, that I can translate
All the magnificence and beauty of these whales!
Such gentleness and yet such strength in their tails.
Working artist magic into their water spout
As best I can—I shout…
Please save the whale!

Now from whimsy to reality…this is the remarkable true story of Coral, the humpback whale

As the Whale and Dolphin Conservation Society's Senior Biologist, I have watched Coral for many years now and have come to think of him as a friend. His story is truly remarkable, one of survival and hope.

Coral was born in 1988 to , Silver, originally called Long John Silver because she was missing half her tail fluke. Coral's life has been marked by tragedy, as a newborn calf he was attacked by orcas, or killer whales, and has several scars, or rake marks, on his fluke as a terrible reminder of this attack.

Photo: WDCS

Three years later in 1991, Coral suffered the loss of his mother, Silver, to entanglement when she was found dead on Long Island. Silver was a very good mother, she had several rake marks on her dorsal fin, most likely acquired through defending Coral.

A year before Coral was born, his sister, Beltane, had also been found dead after eating mackerel contaminated by red algae and was sadly only one of many humpbacks who had met with this awful fate. This is a continuing concern and one that has existed over several years when other red tides were documented.

Despite all of this, Coral has survived to become one of the most sociable whales we have ever observed and, when spotted on whale watches, he is often seen swimming with other whales.

I remember reading the following article in the Cape Cod Times in 2005, which told a remarkable true story of a humpback whale accompanying a dying right whale:

> *"They are an odd couple. A dying right whale, limping along with half a fluke, and a seemingly healthy humpback swimming by her side… it looks like the end is near for an 11-year-old female known only as Right Whale No. 2425… In March, the right whale was hit by a 42-foot recreational vessel off*

Cumberland Island in Georgia… When No. 2425 dies, it will deepen the tragedy that has evolved over the past 10 months in which 5 percent of all reproductively active female right whales have been killed, mostly by humans."

My heart went out to the desperately ill right whale and I was very surprised by the sight of her being accompanied by the humpback, an entirely different species and therefore such an unlikely companion. It was extremely touching how the humpback was keeping the sick right whale company as she slowly made her way and, although it is unknown how such an extraordinary companionship comes about, I was very glad that it had.

As I looked at the photograph, something seemed familiar about the companion humpback whale. At the WDCS, we curate a catalogue of more than 2,000 identifiable humpback whales, with upwards of 200 sightings a year in Massachusetts Bay. Whales are like people in that each is unique. With humpbacks, we therefore identify them by the patterns on the underside of their tail, and also by the serrated edge on top of their fluke. In addition, scars from past experiences, many sadly caused by humans, provide additional identification.

Photo: T. Voorheis

The humpback whale accompanying the dying right whale had a scar behind his blowholes and, as I studied the photograph, I realized that it was Coral! While there is no way of knowing why Coral attended to the right whale in this way, or if he was able to communicate with her, it was a striking irony that he was spending time with a female whale who, like his mother, had lost part of her fluke due to a vessel strike. However, Coral being the sociable whale that he is, it is perhaps not that surprising that he was such a loyal companion to this dying whale.

Another story of survival for Coral occurred in 2005, when he freed himself from entangling fishing gear. Unfortunately, as was the case with Coral's own mother, entanglement is a harsh reality facing many whales and, on discovering Coral was in danger, we had hoped that he would escape the terrible fate that took his mother.

Coral and his family have had to deal with many dangers and life-threatening events, both natural and human-induced, including attacks by Orcas, entanglements, vessel strikes and pollution. Yet his survival should be a beacon of hope to us all, and stand as a reminder to be strong and to keep moving forward even in the face of adversity.

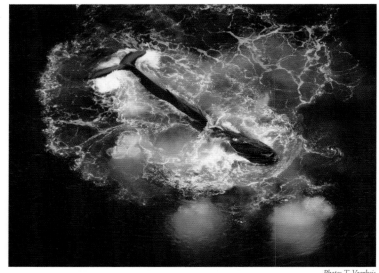

Photo: T. Voorheis

It is on behalf of animals like Coral that, for nearly a quarter-century, the Whale and Dolphin Conservation Society has dedicated itself to:

1. Reducing and, ultimately, eliminating the continuing threats to cetaceans and their habitats.

2. Raising awareness of these wonderful animals and the need for us to protect them in their natural environment.

If you would like to help WDCS protect whales like Coral please phone **508-746-2522** or go to ***http://www.whales.org***

Thank you,

Regina Asmutis-Silvia
WDCS Senior Biologist

Whale and Dolphin Conservation Society

44

The Cape Cod Mermaid Gallery
is proud to offer tee shirts and full-color prints
made from the art appearing on these pages.
Visit www.thecapecodmermaid.com

Tee shirts (white, 100% cotton), available in small, medium, large, extra-large and double-extra-large, $20.00 ea.
(Please specify quantity, size and page number when ordering – example: 1 ea. med. p. 12)

Prints (11" x 17" overall, with color image area of approx. 9" x 12" on a white border), suitable for framing, $36.00 ea.
(Please specify quantity and page number when ordering – example: 2 ea. p. 37)

Also available, books by Theresa LaBrecque:
Tea Time with Mermaids, $19.95 ea,
A Whale of a Good Time, $23.95 ea.

Please add $4.00 per item for shipping and handling in the continental United States (please call for rates to other destinations). Shipments to Massachusetts addresses must also include 5% sales tax.

The Cape Cod Mermaid Gallery
Phone 774-323-0333
www.thecapecodmermaid.com

Wholesale inquiries are welcome!

Theresa LaBrecque was born in Maine, and grew up in the deep woods of New Hampshire. It was in these woods that Theresa's whimsy started to grow. Mounds of grass were seen as fairy houses which Theresa would embellish with lichen and acorn trimmings. Later in life Theresa moved to Cape Cod where she found mermaids in the glittering waters and interpreted them in clay, then later in oil on canvas. It was only natural that Theresa's attention would turn to the many friends of the mermaids and put them into clay and canvas as well. Now, the same fantasy that Theresa used to make fairy houses in her youth is being expressed on the back of whales! Whole villages with sheep grazing and laundry drying on the line can be found on the back of one of Theresa's whales. Flowers grow in profusion, and whimsical activities happen there.

A Whale of a Good Time is Theresa's second book. Her first, *Tea Time with Mermaids* was released in June 2007. Undoubtedly, more will follow.

Theresa LaBrecque lives in Brewster, Massachusetts, with her beloved bull terrier Panda, whom you will find in several of her paintings.